EVEN SCARY THINGS GET THE BLUES

Poems & Illustrations by David Buckner

EVEN SCARY THINGS GET THE BLUES

When you hear the word "scary",
You might think of many things.
You might think of creepy aliens
Or monsters with big wings.
But there's something you don't know –
That scary things get sad,
Sometimes they have good days,
Other days are bad.
Scary things have ups and downs,
They win and often lose.
Everyone gets down sometimes,
Even scary things get the blues.

ON TOP OF MY BED

There's a child on top of my bed
And it's filling me up with dread.
I can't go to sleep,
I think I might weep.
I hope this is just in my head!

A ONE-TOOTHED GOBLIN

This is certainly the truth,
This Goblin has one tooth.
So he better start rushin'
To get to tooth brushin'
Or without a doubt
That tooth will fall out!

THE BOOGEYMAN

I've been waiting in this closet all night
And I don't see any children to fright.
What's that you say?
They went away?
They're staying at a friend's house tonight?!

HEADLESS HUGO

Headless Hugo has no head,
He lost it in a fight.
Headless Hugo cannot find it,
His head's nowhere in sight.
"I'll keep searching on and on,"
That's what he's always said.
The only way that he will stop
Is when he finds his head!

ALIENS AMONG US

Aliens are among us
And I'm sure there's more than a few.
They'll try their best to blend in,
To look like me and you.
I bet they'll do normal things
To mimic normal fellas,
Including going to work
And using their umbrellas.
They'll probably wear our same clothes
And even our same shoes.
We won't be able to spot them,
So they'll walk around as they choose.
Wait! I think I see one now!
I tell you, as I'm smirking,
I don't think that their "blending in"
Is altogether working.

ROBOTS

Robots are made of metal,
Their parts are mostly trusty.
But when they go for a swim
Their parts get mostly rusty!

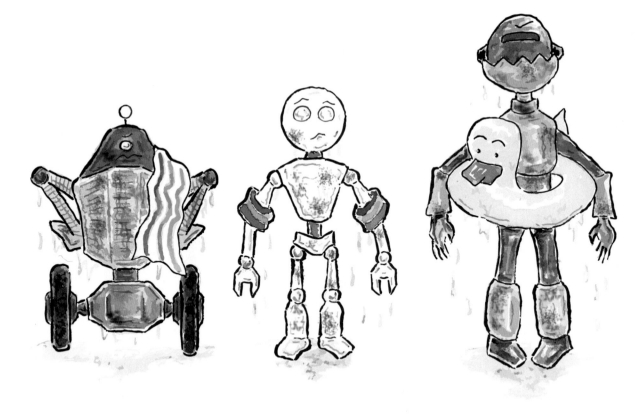

GHOSTS

When it comes to being a ghost,
Your tasks can be very daunting.
Ghosts have to be able to frighten
And always ready for haunting.
So how does a ghost survive
And how does a ghost get by
When it's too afraid to scare
And it's way too nervous and shy?

THE THING THAT HATES WORDS

"I hate every word,
I hate every letter.
If they didn't exist,
The world would be much better.
When I see words,
It's hard to face 'em,
So my instinct is
To simply erase 'em."

THE THING THAT LOVES WORDS

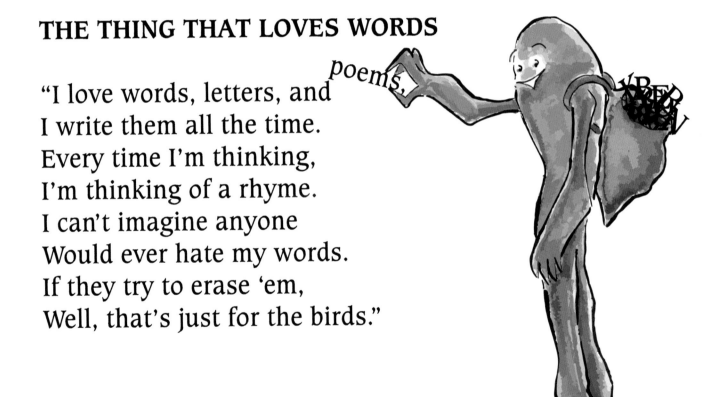

"I love words, letters, and poems,
I write them all the time.
Every time I'm thinking,
I'm thinking of a rhyme.
I can't imagine anyone
Would ever hate my words.
If they try to erase 'em,
Well, that's just for the birds."

THE DILLYGROTH

The slowest beast I've ever seen
Is easily the Dillygroth.
The first time that I saw it,
It was sllooowwweeerrrrrr than a sloth.
Every time it made a move
It went sooo vvveeerrryyy slow.

Did it even move at all?
I guess we'll never know.

IT'S NOT AN EGG

This creature looks like an egg,
But I must shamefully beg,
Don't say it looks like an egg
Or it might just bite your leg!

MONSTER PET

I bought a monster at the store.
It's now my favorite pet.
It started getting big,
So I took it to the vet.
The vet assured me all is fine,
But it continued growing.
I kept on thinking it's okay,
Until its claws started showing.
When I bought my monster pet
It was the size of a mouse.
Now as the days go by
I can't even fit it in my house.

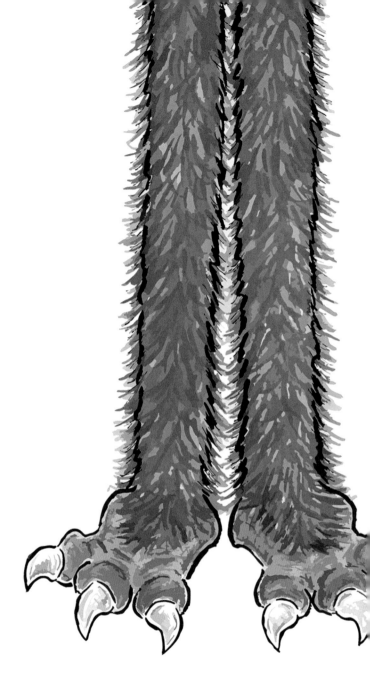

THE WORST DAY OF THE YEAR

I really really hate this day.
I really cannot find a way
To make it fun or make it cool
Because I am a scary ghoul.
On this day I feel so rough,
On this day it's just so tough
To figure out what to be.
Just look at me, you will see.
I'm already ghastly and already green,
So what should I be for Halloween?

THE TWO-HEADED OGRE

This ogre has two heads
And each head has a mind.
When it's time to compromise
It puts them in a bind.
One head likes the color blue,
The other one likes red.
They never agree on anything
So they argue all day instead!

THE GRUCKY

When someone sees a Grucky,
It means that they're unlucky.
It's the biggest and ruddiest,
The grossest and cruddiest.
Its crusty skin is colored red,
With horns all over its nasty head.
Its body is covered with scales
And it has not one, but three tails!
Its heart is full of so much hate,
And when it sees you it's too late!
There's really nothing that you can do,
And it's standing right behind YOU!

THE INVISIBLE CREATURE

If you've ever wondered
Or ever had a hunch
About this creature's diet
And what it's had for lunch,
You shouldn't have to ask it,
You will not have to pry.
Just look right at its belly,
You'll see the reason why.
You can see right through it
And see it didn't eat a bat.
In fact, I'm quite convinced
That I see my neighbor's cat.

THE FLIGHTLESS FLEPTO

Try as you may, try as you might,
You'll never see the Flepto in flight.
It will not fly, it will not soar,
It will not get up off the floor.
Flying gives it many frights
Because the Flepto's scared of heights.

MAKING A WITCH'S BREW

No eye of newt? Just substitute!
A carrot here, some celery there.
No toad in it? Don't throw a fit.
Add potatoes and maybe tomatoes.
Oh, what a shame, got no wolf's bane?
Maybe it's time to add some thyme.
Actually, this might not be
A witch's brew, but vegetable stew!

THE SLIMY SOBBLEWOG

The Slimy Sobblewog will always give you chase,
While scaring you with its slimy face.
Run for your life as you think it wants to beat you,
Scream all you will as you think it wants to eat you.
But honestly it doesn't mean to bug you,
In reality it only wants to hug you!

A TEA PARTY WITH BIGFOOT

A tea party can be fun,
But please don't invite Bigfoot.
Because when he sits down
His chair will go kaput!

AN OLD CYCLOPS

An old cyclops needed glasses,
So he went looking for a pair.
He couldn't find any that fit him
Because his situation was so rare.
These glasses aren't working out,
He has no idea what to do.
He was born with just one eye
And glasses are made for two.

HEADLESS HUGO FOUND A HEAD

Headless Hugo found a head,
This head fits him just right.
Headless Hugo really loves it,
He thinks it's out of sight.
"I think it's time to end my search,"
He'd like you all to know.
But don't tell him his head will melt
Because it's made of snow!

A ZOMBIE'S DILEMMA

I tried to change my diet,
But my mind just wouldn't buy it.
I took a chance at human food,
It only made me mean and rude.
I finally thought I just might try
Something that's called pizza pie.
It wasn't good, not even close.
In fact it was downright gross.
The simple fact always remains
That I'm always craving brains.

BABY MONSTERS

When baby monsters are born,
They begin like we all do.
They have to learn everything
From their parents too.
They have to learn to crawl,
Then they learn to walk.
They start off making sounds
And eventually learn to talk.
Someday they'll get older
And they'll be fully grown.
They'll move out of the house
To live life on their own.

Made in the USA
Lexington, KY
03 June 2019